USBORNE BIG MACHINES
TRACTORS

Caroline Young

Designed by Steve Page

Illustrated by Chris Lyon and Teri Gower

Consultant: Mick Roberts
(Machinery Editor, Farmers Weekly)

Contents

Tractors

Tractors have to do many different jobs on a farm and can work in all sorts of weather.

Farmers drive them over bumpy, muddy fields, so they have to be tough and hard-wearing.

This is the tractor's cab, where the driver sits.

This is the tractor's engine. It is powerful, but does not use much fuel.

Tractors can go on roads but they cannot move as fast as cars or trucks.

When these lights are switched on, the tractor can even work at night.

Tractors need tough, thick tires.

The main part of the tractor is called the chassis.

This light flashes when the tractor drives on roads. Other drivers see it and slow down.

This back window opens to let fresh air into the cab in hot weather.

The cab has a heater for cold weather.

Tractors can easily tip over if they drive up very steep slopes. These metal bars stop the farmer from getting crushed if that happens.

Tractors can turn around in small spaces. They must not squash crops in the fields.

Mud and bumps

Tractor tires have deep grooves in them. They grip wet, muddy ground without getting stuck.

A tractor's body is high above the wheels, to stop damage from rocky, bumpy ground.

Its powerful engine keeps the tractor going up any sloping ground around the farm, too.

Three links

Tractors pull many different farming tools behind them.

The tools are fastened to three metal links behind the cab. A metal pole called a Power Take-Off (P.T.O.) carries power from the tractor's engine to the tools. This makes them work.

P.T.O.

Three links

Tractors at work

A tractor's main job is driving up and down fields, pulling farming tools. The four tools on this page get the ground ready for crops to grow.

Plow

This tractor is pulling a plow. Plows break up and turn over hard, flat earth. They also bury weeds. This makes the ground better for planting seeds in.

Metal blades called coulters cut straight down into the ground.

These blades are called shares. They slice under the earth cut by the coulters.

At the edge of the field, the tractor lifts the plow and turns around. Then, it lowers the plow ready to start another furrow.

This board turns the sliced earth over. It is called the mouldboard.

This small ditch made by the plow is called a furrow.

Harrow

This tractor is pulling a harrow. Harrowing breaks down the big slices of earth the plow has made.

This type of harrow is called a disc harrow.

These rows of metal discs break down clods of earth as they are pulled over it.

This harrow has over 35 discs. They are arranged in rows called gangs.

Gang

The gangs are spread out behind the tractor to harrow more earth.

This metal bar is called a shaft. The harrow's discs are attached to it.

Roller

This roller smooths the earth after harrowing. It makes the field level for planting seeds in.

Each of these rollers is made up of 20 steel rings.

A tractor can roll a field quickly with wide rollers. It has to make fewer trips up and down it.

Stones can damage farm machines. The rollers press them into the ground.

Seed drill

Now the field is ready for seeds to be planted in it. This tractor is pulling a seed drill which does that job.

The drill makes grooves in the earth. Seeds drop down into them.

Seeds are held in this box. It is called a hopper.

These spikes cover the planted seeds with earth.

Spreaders and sprayers

Crops need food called fertilizer to grow well. They may need protection from insects and diseases, too. The machines on this page spread fertilizer over fields or spray them with pest-killing chemicals.

Manure spreader

Farm animals produce a lot of waste. It is called manure or dung. It is a very good fertilizer.

A tractor pulls this machine to spread manure over crops. It is called a manure spreader.

This tool is called a grab (see page 14). It fills the spreader with manure.

As the tractor moves, its P.T.O. (Power Take-Off) pulls four chains along the floor of the spreader.

Chains carry the manure to the back of the machine.

These spiked wheels chop up the manure. They are called shredders.

The shredders spread a layer of chopped manure onto the field by flinging it out of the back of the spreader.

Sprayer

Some farmers spray fields with chemicals called pesticides to kill insects and diseases. They are poisonous, so farmers must use them very carefully.

The machine attached to this tractor is called a sprayer. As the tractor moves, it sprays out exactly the right amount of pesticide.

Super sprayers

In some countries, fields are huge. Farmers attach very wide sprayers behind their tractors to spray their land as quickly as possible. This sprayer is about as long as two buses.

This is an extra tank of pesticide.

Farmers do not spray pesticides on windy days. The chemicals must not blow around.

This is called the boom. It is the main part of the spraying machine.

This tank holds the pesticide mixed with some water.

The mixture is pumped through these pipes.

A pump pushes pesticide out of these tiny holes, called nozzles.

This boom has more than 20 nozzles.

7

Combine harvester

This farming machine is called a combine harvester. It combines two jobs in one machine. First, it cuts and gathers up crops such as wheat, peas and barley. This is called harvesting. Then it separates grains from their stalks. This is called threshing. Here you can see how it works.

Sorting out

Many crops are stalks with grains at the top. A combine cuts and pulls in the whole stalk.

Inside the cab

Some combine harvesters have computers in the cab. They tell the driver how full the grain tank is and how well the machine is working.

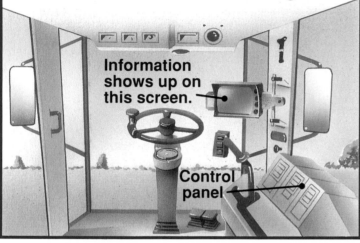

Information shows up on this screen.

Control panel

Metal teeth at the front of the combine push through the field. They divide it into strips.

A blade cuts the stalks off at the bottom. It makes about 1,000 cuts a minute.

This wheel, called a reel, spins around. It is covered with metal spikes called tines.

The tines push the cut stalks into the combine harvester.

Inside the machine, a stone trap catches any stones.

Drum

Box

Inside the combine, a spinning drum shakes the grains off the stalks. They collect in a box.

Chaff

Straw

The stalks are pushed out of the back as straw. Fans blow out waste bits called chaff.

Trailer

The grain is unloaded into a trailer. A tractor will pull it to a dry barn to be stored.

When the tank is full, grain is pushed into a trailer by this moving screw.

D

A scooping machine carries the grain up into this box, called the grain tank.

The grain falls down onto this metal sheet. It is called the grain pan.

These metal trays are called straw walkers. They shake any grains that are left off the stalks.

This conveyor belt carries the crop into a spinning drum. Most of the grains drop off their stalks in there.

Hay and straw

Farmers use these machines to cut and gather hay and straw. Straw is used as bedding for farm animals. Hay is dried grass, which they eat.

Mower

This tractor is pulling a grass mower. The mower cuts grass and leaves it in rows called swaths on the field.

These blades spin around about 3,000 times in a minute. They cut the grass.

Swath

Power from the tractor's P.T.O. goes through this metal arm to make the blades turn.

Swath turner

Straw and grass must be completely dry before they are made into bundles called bales. This tool is called a swath turner. It helps dry swaths out by turning them over.

These are swath boards. They can move in or out to make thinner or fatter swaths.

These wheels are called finger wheels. They pick up grass in the swath and turn it over.

Baler

Wrapping hay and straw into bales makes it easier to carry them around. This machine makes round bales. It is called a round baler.

How it works

Drum

Bale

Metal fingers at the front of the baler push hay and straw into the machine. Spinning drums roll them into a ball.

String ties the bale up tight. Then the top half of the baler opens. The new bale falls out of the back onto the field.

Straw and hay are pushed up into here as the baler moves forward.

These drums spin around. They roll the hay and straw up into a bale.

Bale chamber

This strong string called twine ties the bales up.

The bale falls out of the back of the baler.

These metal fingers are called the pick-up. They push hay and straw up into the bale chamber.

Feeding animals

In the summer, animals can eat grass or crops grown for them. This sort of animal food is called forage. Farmers harvest forage crops in the summer and make them into a food called silage. They can feed this to their animals in winter, when less forage grows.

Forage to silage

Forage harvester   **Trailer**

Trailer   **Dumpbox**

Silo   **Blower**

The forage harvester picks up cut grass. It chops it up and blows it into a trailer.

The chopped-up forage is tipped into a metal box called a dumpbox back in the farmyard.

A blower blows forage into a tower called a silo. Inside here, it slowly becomes silage.

Forage harvester

This machine is a forage harvester. It picks up forage crops and chops them up as it moves.

This is the pick-up. It spins around very fast, picking up forage with metal spikes called tines.

The spinning cutterhead is like a fast fan. It blows the forage up this spout into the trailer.

This is the cutterhead. It has 15 steel knives, which chop forage as the cutterhead whizzes around.

Dumpbox and blower

At one end of the dumpbox, a blower blows forage into the tower silo with a powerful fan. Inside the silo, forage pickles as if it was in vinegar. This turns it into silage.

A silo must be completely sealed. No air must get in. This makes forage pickle better.

The silo is sealed shut all summer while the forage becomes silage.

A moving metal belt carries the forage up to the other end of the dumpbox.

It is dangerous to go into a silo. Silage gives off smelly gases so there is no air inside for humans to breathe.

These toothed wheels turn around. They push the forage towards the blower.

This is the blower. It needs power from a tractor's P.T.O. to make it work.

The forage is blown very fast up this pipe.

It takes about 45 minutes to blow all the silage out of the dumpbox into the silo.

 # Lifters

Tools can be attached to the front and back of tractors. These tools are specially built to lift and carry around the farm.

Grab

This tool is called a grab. The farmer can fasten it to his tractor to pick up and move silage or manure.

This is the grab.

These prongs are called tines. They are arranged like rows of teeth.

The tractor driver controls the grab with levers inside the cab.

These extra tines stop anything from falling out of the side of the grab.

How the grab works

Tines

When the grab is near the manure, the driver pulls a lever. Its tines open up like a mouth.

Another lever makes the tines close around some manure. The grab lifts up with its load.

The tines open to let the manure fall out where the driver wants to unload it.

Bale fork

Bales of hay and straw are heavy and difficult to lift. Farmers fasten a tool called a bale fork to their tractor to move them around the farm.

This spike sticks deep into the bale.

This metal pedal pushes the bale off the spikes.

This smaller spike stops the bale swaying from side to side as the tractor drives along.

Fork-lift tractor

Farmers need to move sacks of grain, cattle food or fertilizer around the farm. They can fasten a fork-lift to the front of a tractor to do this.

Boom

These two prongs are called forks. They are on the end of a metal arm called a boom. Together, they make the fork-lift.

Sacks rest on wooden trays laid on top of the forks.

How it works

Bale

Fork

As the tractor moves forward, the fork sticks into the bale.

The bale fork lifts up to carry loads, so that the farmer can see the road.

Pedal

The tractor lowers the bale fork. A pedal pushes the bale off.

Root crop machines

Farmers use these machines to plant and harvest vegetables such as potatoes and carrots. We eat their roots, so they are called root crops.

Potato planter

This is an automatic potato planter. It plants small potatoes, called seed potatoes, under the ground as it moves.

This box is called the hopper. It can hold 30 sacks of seed potatoes.

The seed potatoes fall into grooves called furrows in the field.

These metal blades are called ridging plows. They cover the seed potatoes with earth.

Chains drag over the earth to make nicely shaped ridges.

Root crop harvester

This is a root crop harvester. It is harvesting potatoes.

Blades called shares slice under the potatoes. They lift the whole plant out of the ground.

The tractor guides the harvester between the rows of potato plants.

Inside the machine

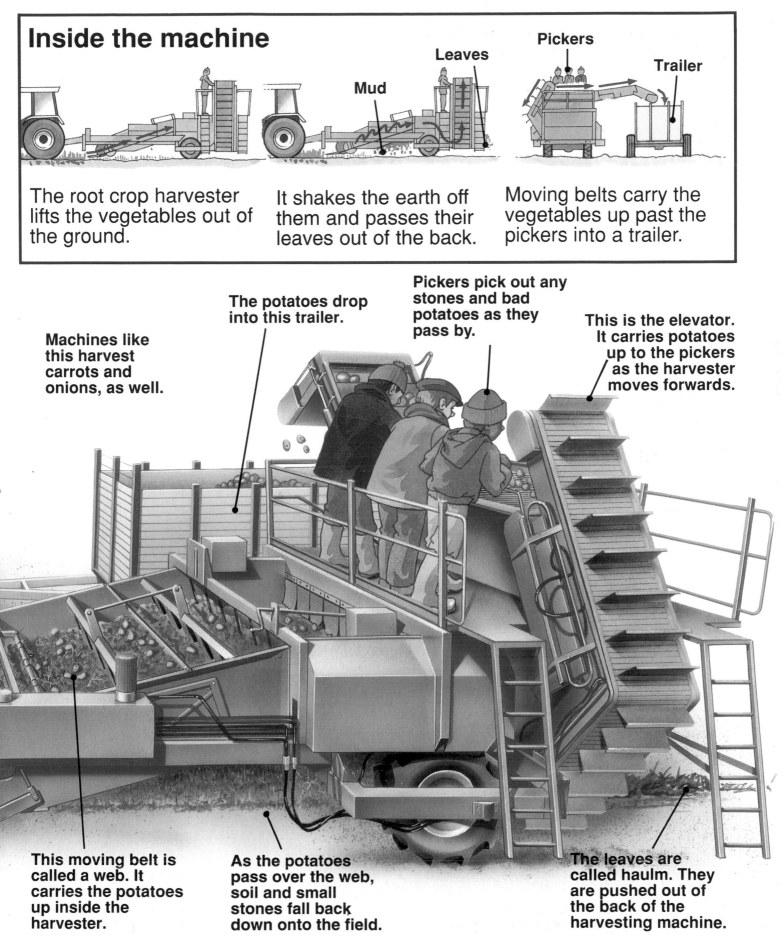

Mud

Leaves

Pickers

Trailer

The root crop harvester lifts the vegetables out of the ground.

It shakes the earth off them and passes their leaves out of the back.

Moving belts carry the vegetables up past the pickers into a trailer.

The potatoes drop into this trailer.

Pickers pick out any stones and bad potatoes as they pass by.

This is the elevator. It carries potatoes up to the pickers as the harvester moves forwards.

Machines like this harvest carrots and onions, as well.

This moving belt is called a web. It carries the potatoes up inside the harvester.

As the potatoes pass over the web, soil and small stones fall back down onto the field.

The leaves are called haulm. They are pushed out of the back of the harvesting machine.

 # Giant tractor

Ordinary tractors are not powerful enough for some farming jobs. Huge machines like this do them. This tractor usually works in the big wheat fields of North America. It can work for a long time without stopping.

Wheels and weight

Tractors like this are very heavy. They need eight wheels to carry their enormous weight.

All eight tires turn together to make the huge tractor move and turn around.

The tractor's tires are very wide. This helps them grip more ground to pull the tractor along.

Giant tractors like this are heavy and slow. They can only go about as fast as a bicycle.

This tractor can pull heavy loads and other farming tools behind it, too.

Headlights

Big Bud

This is one of the biggest tractors in the world. It is called Big Bud. Its tires are taller than a man.

Big Bud was specially built to work on big farms in North America.

These eight wide tires spread the tractor's weight out over more ground. They help stop it from sinking into the field.

This tractor can work for about 24 hours without needing more fuel.

This is the air filter. It stops dust from getting into the engine and damaging it.

Sitting in this cab is like looking out of an upstairs window of a house.

The driver can listen to the radio or cassettes while he works long hours.

Giant tractors often work at night, too. They have lights at the front and at the back.

This thick glass stops too much engine noise from getting into the cab.

Some of the wheat fields in North America are so long that it can take an hour to drive from one end to the other.

This tractor's engine is much more powerful than an ordinary tractor's engine.

Loaders

These machines are built to pick up loads. They are called loaders. Three different types of loaders work on farms.

Tractor loader

This is a tractor loader. It has a bucket used for scooping things into attached in front of its cab.

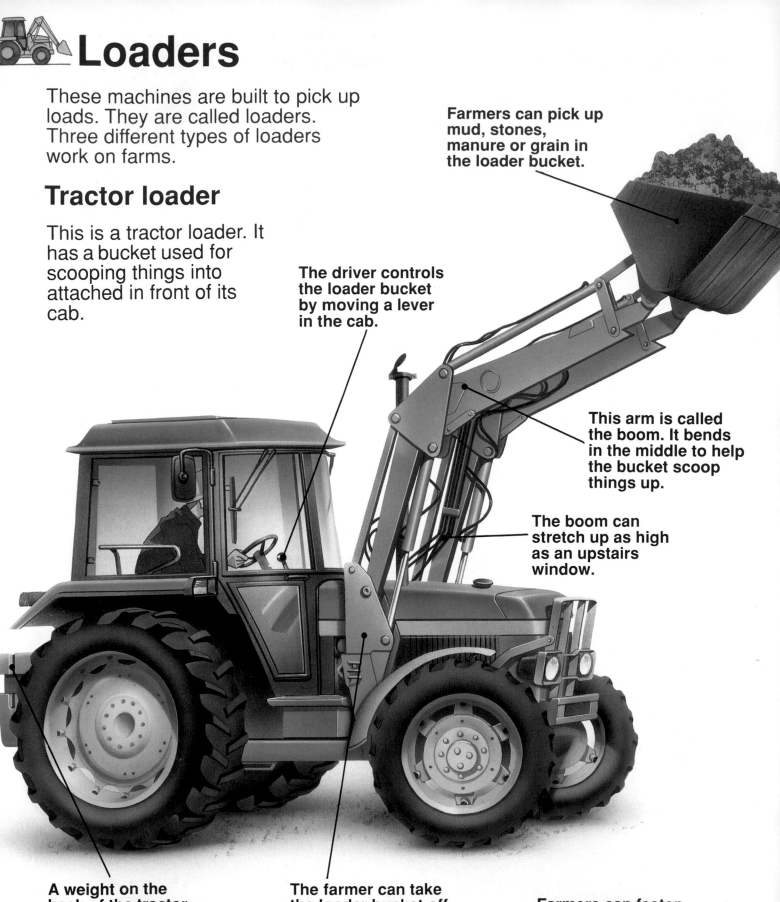

Farmers can pick up mud, stones, manure or grain in the loader bucket.

The driver controls the loader bucket by moving a lever in the cab.

This arm is called the boom. It bends in the middle to help the bucket scoop things up.

The boom can stretch up as high as an upstairs window.

A weight on the back of the tractor stops it falling forward when it carries heavy loads. It is called the counterweight.

The farmer can take the loader bucket off the tractor in only a few minutes.

Farmers can fasten other tools to the front of loaders. You can see some on pages 14 and 15.

Skid-steer loader

This skid-steer loader does smaller loading jobs. It is called a skid-steer loader because it can turn around so quickly and easily it is like skidding.

Telescopic loader

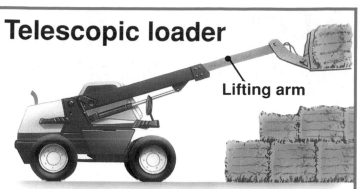

Lifting arm

Loaders like this are called telescopic loaders. On these machines, the lifting arm slides out from inside a straight metal case, just like a telescope does.

The driver sits in this small cab.

Metal bars called rollbars protect him in case the loader topples over.

Skid-steer loaders can stop and spin around to face the other way in a very small space.

The driver controls the loader with foot pedals in the cab.

Lift and load

Bucket

Boom

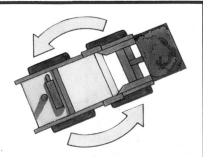

A skid-steer loader can scoop things up when its bucket tilts like this.

Its boom can reach up and unload things high above the cab.

The farmer can steer the loader so that it turns around in a circle.

Around the farm

Tractors do many unusual jobs on a farm. Here, they have tools fastened to them for digging ditches, cutting hedges and banging in fence posts.

Ditch digger

If a field stays too wet after rain, crops cannot grow in it. The farmer must get the water off the field, or drain it.

This tractor is using a tool called a backhoe to dig drainage ditches. The water will flow off the field and into the ditches.

Hedge-trimmer

Farmers have to keep hedges tidy. This tractor has an arm called a hedge-trimmer fixed to it. As the tractor moves, the trimmer's metal blades cut the tops off hedges.

The backhoe has its own seat. It faces backwards so the farmer can see where he is digging.

These are the controls for the bucket.

The digging arm can move up and down or from side to side.

The backhoe's bucket has metal teeth along its edge. They can cut through hard earth.

Metal legs stop the tractor from toppling over backward as it digs.

This frame fastens the backhoe and its seat to the back of the tractor.

Post driver

Tractors can help the farmer put fences around his fields. This tractor has a tool called a post driver attached to it. It pushes fence posts into the ground. The farmer joins them up with wire.

This metal frame fastens the post driver to the back of the tractor. It is very strong.

This heavy weight is like a hammer. It bangs the posts into the ground.

Pushing power

Post

The farmer slides a wooden post into a slot in the post driver.

He puts the post driver above the place where he wants a fence post.

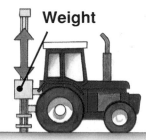

Weight

Heavy weights slide down the driver and bang the post into the ground.

Some frames can swing around to work on either side of the tractor.

This post driver can bash in a post every 40 seconds.

Post

Post drivers are sometimes called post bashers.

These metal legs are called stabilizers. They hold the tractor steady as it thumps in posts.

Crawler tractor

This tractor has rubber tracks instead of tires. They are called crawler tracks. Farmers use crawler tractors like this in wet, muddy fields where ordinary tractors might get stuck.

They can also pull heavy loads and farming tools without their tracks slipping or sinking.

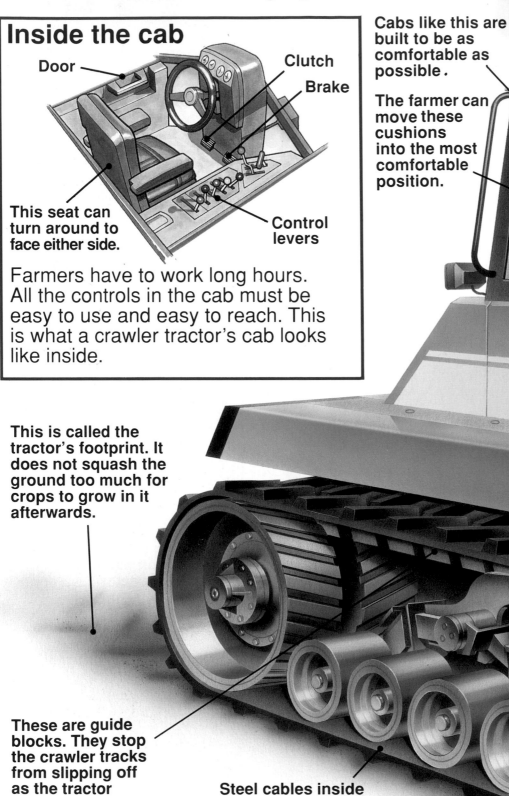

Inside the cab

Door

Clutch

Brake

This seat can turn around to face either side.

Control levers

Farmers have to work long hours. All the controls in the cab must be easy to use and easy to reach. This is what a crawler tractor's cab looks like inside.

Cabs like this are built to be as comfortable as possible.

The farmer can move these cushions into the most comfortable position.

This is called the tractor's footprint. It does not squash the ground too much for crops to grow in it afterwards.

These are guide blocks. They stop the crawler tracks from slipping off as the tractor moves.

Steel cables inside this rubber track make it stronger.

24

The cab can be made cooler or warmer.

Tinted glass stops bright sunshine from getting into the driver's eyes.

Crawler combine

Sometimes, combine harvesters have crawler tracks too. Farmers can use them to harvest crops in very wet fields, where ordinary combines cannot easily move.

When the driver turns the steering wheel in the cab, the tracks turn smoothly in any direction.

The tractor's engine is under here.

This tractor has 12 gears for different speeds. But it can never go very fast.

These rubber tracks have ridges called lugs, as tractor tires do. They grip the ground well.

Fruit-farming machines

Farmers who grow fruit need different sorts of farming machines. You can see two of them here.

Berry harvester

Fruit can easily be damaged when it is picked. Then it is not worth as much money.

This machine harvests grapes and berries without squashing them.

Looking inside

Prongs　　**Discs**

The branches of each bush are pushed into two halves by metal prongs and plastic discs.

Tray　　**Fingers**

Plastic fingers above the discs gently tap each bush. Berries drop off into trays.

Picker

The trays slowly move, carrying the berries up to pickers. They pack the fruit into boxes.

The driver drives the machine very slowly over the bushes.

These plastic fingers knock the berries off.

The bushes push these flexible discs back as they go into the machine.

These metal prongs part the bush into two, like hair.

The berries are slowly carried up here on a moving belt.

The picker fills plastic boxes with berries. When one is full, he stacks it up while the other picker fills a box.

Mistblower

This is a mistblower. It is specially built to spray tall fruit trees and grape vines with chemicals that kill insects and diseases.

Trees and vines are too tall for ordinary sprayers, like the one on page 7, to reach them.

This is the tank. It holds the chemical mixture.

The leaves and dirt fall out of the bottom of the machine.

This fan behind the tank pushes the mixture out of pipes, called hoses.

The hoses can be attached at different heights, so they spray every bit of the plant.

27

Special tractors

Farmers need different tractors for different jobs. The ones on this page are built to do special sorts of work.

Three-wheeler

This tractor has three huge wheels. They hold so much air that the tractor does not squash the soil.

Its job is to spread fertilizer over big fields just before seeds are planted in them.

This tractor's cab is much higher above the ground than on ordinary tractors.

This light flashes when the tractor is moving on roads.

This trailer is full of fertilizer.

These big, round tires spread the tractor's weight over the field.

The engine is under the cab, not in front of it. This means that all three wheels help spread out its weight.

Mini-tractor

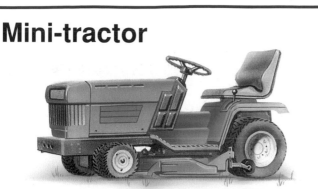

This tractor is too small for farm-work. People use mini-tractors like this to mow the grass on golf-courses, in parks or in large gardens.

Narrow tractor

Tractors like this can work between rows of grapevines or fruit trees. They are very narrow, so that they don't damage any crops.

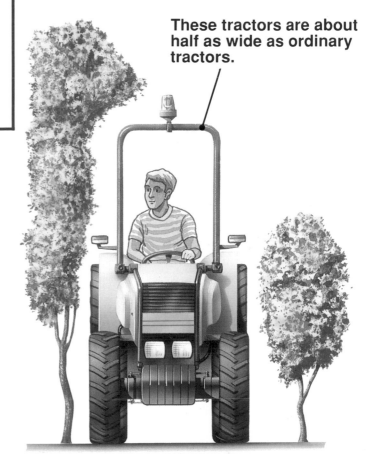

These tractors are about half as wide as ordinary tractors.

These tires are more than twice as wide as ordinary tractor tires.

A.T.V.

This A.T.V. can go as fast as an ordinary motorbike.

Some farmers ride around their fields on bikes like these. They are called A.T.V.s. This is short for All-Terrain Vehicle, which means they can go over any sort of ground.

Tractors old and new

Farming has changed a lot in the last 100 years. Tractors and other farming machines make the farmer's job much easier than it used to be.

On these two pages you can see some of the first tractors, as well as some of the newest farm machines that work in the fields today.

Early tractor

This tractor was built in Canada around 80 years ago. At that time, more and more farmers started using machines to do their farm-work.

This tractor uses a fuel called kerosene to make it work.

These wheels are made of solid metal. They have ridges cut into them to help them to grip, though.

This type of tractor can use gas in its engine.

Three wheeler

This tractor was built in 1914. It only has three wheels. It was popular because it was tough and cheap to run.

This tractor is called 'The Bull'.

Lighter tractor

By the 1930s, many tractors looked like this. They have rubber tires. These are lighter than metal ones are which makes tractors easier to drive.

Rubber tires grip the ground better than metal wheels.

Systems tractor

This machine works on many farms in Europe today. It is called a systems tractor. Farmers fasten tools to the front, middle and back of it, so it can do three jobs at once.

The seed drill plants seeds in the ground.

This trailer spreads fertilizers onto the field.

This systems tractor needs a big engine to push all these tools through the ground.

The tractor has a powerful sort of harrow fixed to the front. It gets the soil ready for planting.

Gantry

This wide machine is called a gantry. It farms big fields without squashing the soil by making too many trips up and down it.

The driver sits in this cab. He has a clear view of the field and the gantry as he drives.

Some gantries are as long as six men lying down head to toe.

Gantries are often used by farmers who grow flowers. This sort of farming is called horticulture.

Index